TOPSY &
LEARN TO
HORSE RIDE

Jean and Gareth Adamson

Blackie

We should like to thank Mrs Shirley Reeder,
staff and ponies at Grove Farm Riding School,
Workington, Suffolk, for all their kind help
in preparing this book.

Blackie and Son Limited
7 Leicester Place
London WC2H 7BP

Printed in Great Britain by
Thomson Litho Ltd, East Kilbride, Scotland

When Topsy and Tim went to watch
the Pony Club Gymkhana they had
a big surprise. One of the riders
was their friend Josie Miller.

'Well done, Josie,' said Dad.
'Where did you learn to ride
like that?'
'At Mrs Reed's Riding School,'
said Josie.

Mrs Reed was at the Gymkhana too,
helping with the ponies. Mummy
went to talk to her.
'Are Topsy and Tim too young to
have riding lessons?' asked Mummy.

'What do you think, Topsy and Tim?' said Mrs Reed. 'Would you like to have riding lessons?'

'Yes *please*,' said Topsy and Tim.

'I have a beginners' class every Thursday,' Mrs Reed told Mummy. 'Topsy and Tim are just right for that.'

'What should the twins wear for riding?' asked Mummy. Mrs Reed said they must wear hard hats, just in case of accidents.
'Shall we wear our wellies?' said Topsy, looking at Josie's smart boots.
'No,' said Mrs Reed. 'Sturdy, leather shoes are much safer. Wellingtons are too loose and floppy.'

'Just one more thing,' said Mrs Reed.
'I hope you know your left from your
right.' Topsy and Tim wondered why.

'Do you know your left and right?'
asked Dad on the way home.
'This is my left,' said Topsy.
'That's right,' said Dad.
'And this is my right,' said Tim.
'No,' said Dad. 'That's wrong.'

It was a long wait until their
first riding lesson but at
last Thursday came.
Mrs Reed took Topsy and Tim to
the stables to meet their ponies.
Topsy's pony was called George.
A big girl called Julie was
there to look after George and
Topsy.

Tim's pony was called Gipsy and
Sally was there to look after
Gipsy and Tim.
Gipsy nibbled at Tim's hair.
'Stop it, Gipsy. That's hair,
not hay,' said Sally.

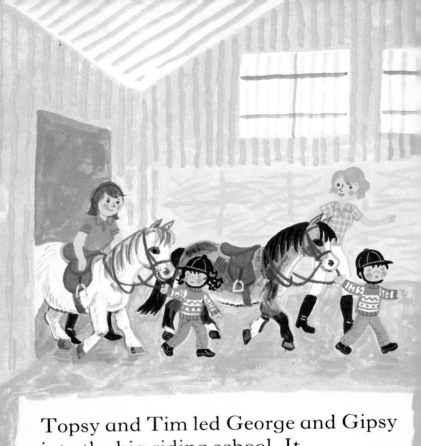

Topsy and Tim led George and Gipsy
into the big riding school. It
wasn't like Topsy and Tim's Primary
School. It was an enormous barn,
with soft, dry earth on the floor.

There were some more children there,
already on their ponies.

Julie helped Topsy to mount George.
'First put your left foot up into
the stirrup,' she said.
'What would happen if I put my right
foot up first?' asked Topsy.
'You'd end up back to front on the
pony,' laughed Julie.

It was nice being up on the ponies. Topsy and Tim felt quite safe with Sally and Julie beside them.

Mrs Reed explained to Topsy and Tim how to start their ponies with a squeeze from their legs, how to use the reins to guide the ponies and how to stop them by gently pulling on the reins.

Tim gave Gipsy a squeeze with his
legs, but nothing happened.
'Squeeze a bit harder,' said Sally.
Tim gave a bonk with both legs—
and Gipsy started walking.
'Well done Tim,' said Mrs Reed.

'Now make your ponies trot,' said
Mrs Reed. The ponies began to trot
quite fast. Topsy and Tim were
bounced up and down on their saddles.
'Ow! Ow! Ow!' said Topsy.

They had to learn to rise up and down, to miss the bumps.
'You *are* doing well,' said Mrs Reed.
'I don't think Topsy and Tim *are* beginners, they're doing so well!'

Topsy and Tim pulled their reins
to stop their ponies. Now they
had to balance without
stirrups . . . put their hands on
their heads . . . shut their eyes . . .
reach right forward to touch their
ponies' heads . . . and right back
to touch their tails.
It was fun!

They ended with games and a race
across the riding school. Sally
and Julie were quite breathless.

Their first riding lesson was over.
Topsy and Tim dismounted.
'My legs feel all wibbly-wobbly,'
said Tim.
'So do mine,' said Topsy.

They took the ponies back to their stables and helped to take their saddles and bridles off. Tim patted Gipsy's mane and stroked her neck. Topsy gave George hugs and kisses. George looked very pleased.

Topsy and Tim fell asleep on the
drive back home, but they woke up
in time for tea. After tea Josie
came to play in the garden.
Dad looked out of the window.
'There are three ponies in our
garden!' he shouted. Mummy ran
to look. 'They are called Topsy
and Tim and Josie,' laughed Dad.